Jack and the Weedstalk

by Roger Mee Senseless

Once upon a time there was a boy called Jack. Jack lived with his mum, Sharon, in a not very nice place called Grimsville. They were quite poor, with very little to call their own. In fact, they only had one thing of any real value... Inexplicably, a cow.

"Mum, why do we have a cow when we live on the 14th floor of a tower block?" asked Jack one day.

"Your stupid twat of a dad bought it in a pub. They told him that it was a dog and he was such a dipshit that he believed it."

A GUIDE FOR DOG BUYERS

a dog

woof

a dog

bark

MOOOO

not a dog

It was, indeed, a very impractical pet. The cow (who was called Nigel) liked to leave shit bombs all over the carpet and the small box room of the flat had been classed as a no-go zone. The neighbours had no idea that it was there but must've wondered where the stench was coming from. Getting it in the lift to take it for a walk was also pretty problematic.

"That's it, I've had enough of this. Nigel has got to go!" said Sharon one day.

"Jack, take the cow down to the market and sell it for as much as you can get for it. Then on the way back buy me 200 scratch cards and however many king sized fags you can afford. And stop giving me those cow eyes, Nigel. It's time to return you to nature, you've been cooped up in here too long. Or the abattoir, whichever pays better."

"Mum, I can't buy your fags. I'm underage," protested Jack.

"Not this again, put on a deep voice, stand on a box or sit on your friend's shoulders with a long trench coat hiding him, that always works in the cartoons. Whatever. USE YOUR INITIATIVE!"

"Put on a deep voice? I'm only 7."

"Stop your whinging and get it done!"

"But why can't you go mum?"

"Because Homes Under the Hammer is on and I've only seen this one 4 times, you cheeky little git."

And so, Jack found himself after much struggle, outside the front of his tower block holding Nigel the cow by a lead that was fashioned from an old skipping rope. The market was 3 miles away so he put his head down and started walking.

When he eventually arrived at the market everyone was already packing up. Jack approached the only person who was still trading. "Excuse me, would you like to buy a lovely, pedigree cow. It's only had one owner, it's very low mileage and has full service history."

Jack, thinking he'd been pretty smart, had read up on some selling tips from a website called 'AutoTrader' before he'd left the flat.

He would've taken the cow to

WEBUYANYCOW.COM

but everyone knew that they were rip off bastards.

"Hmm, that's quite tempting," said the man. "But I'm afraid I've got a bit of a cash flow problem at the moment. Would you accept a swap for him?"

"I don't know," said Jack. "What have you got?"

"Well, I've got this," said the man. He showed Jack a gold watch, with what looked like diamonds stuck around the edge of the face, held in with blu-tac. "It's a completely authentic, 99% genuine Rolex."

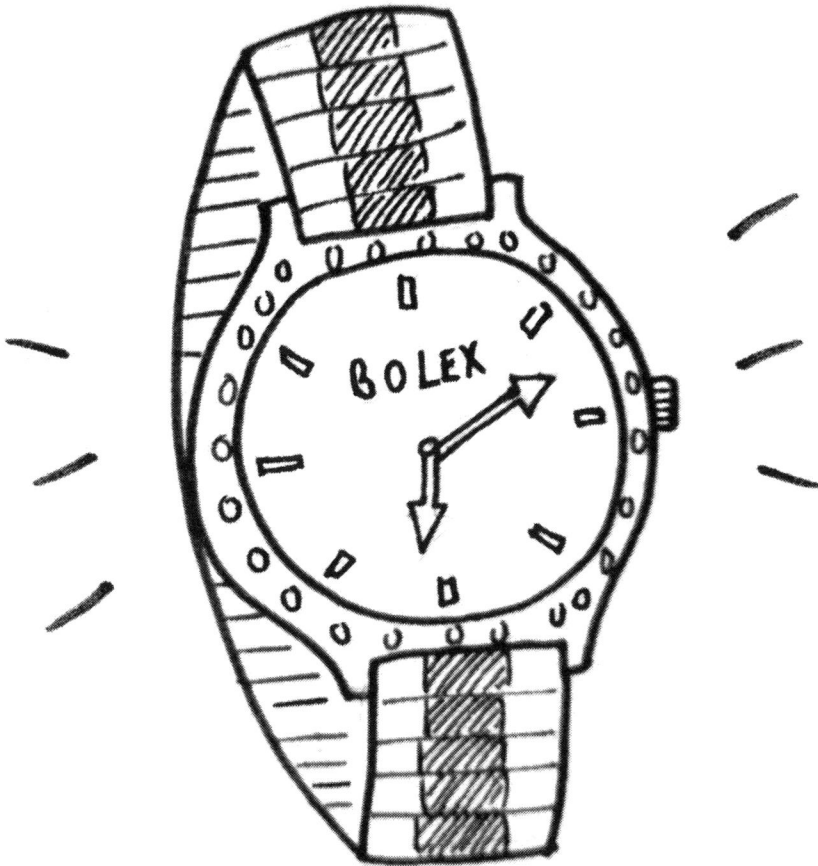

"And, what's more, it's a super rare one because the 'R' in Rolex has been mis-printed so it's actually a 'B', see?"

The man thrust the watch into Jack's face but kept moving it around so Jack couldn't really focus on it.

"It's really accurate, you only have to reset the time every 7 hours. It must be worth at least a bazillion pounds. At least."

"That's tempting," said Jack. "But have you got anything else?"

"No not really, I tell you what. How about I just buy part of it? I'll give you the watch and a packet of sweets for the two back legs?"

Jack considered this.

"I don't think that's going to work. It took me half the day to get here. How long is it going to take me to get a 2 legged cow home?"

"Yeh, I see your problem there," said the man. "Let me go an see what I've got in the back of the van."

The man rooted around inside his van for anything that he could trade. The dashboard was covered in old copies of the Daily Star and McDonald's and KFC wrappers. Inside the glovebox he found what he was looking for. It was a small packet of what he thought were broad beans. He grabbed a felt tip pen and wrote the words 'MAJICK BEANS' onto the packet.

"Here you go," said the man. "These beans are absolutely worthless, sorry I mean priceless. Plant these and they will make you rich beyond your wildest dreams!"

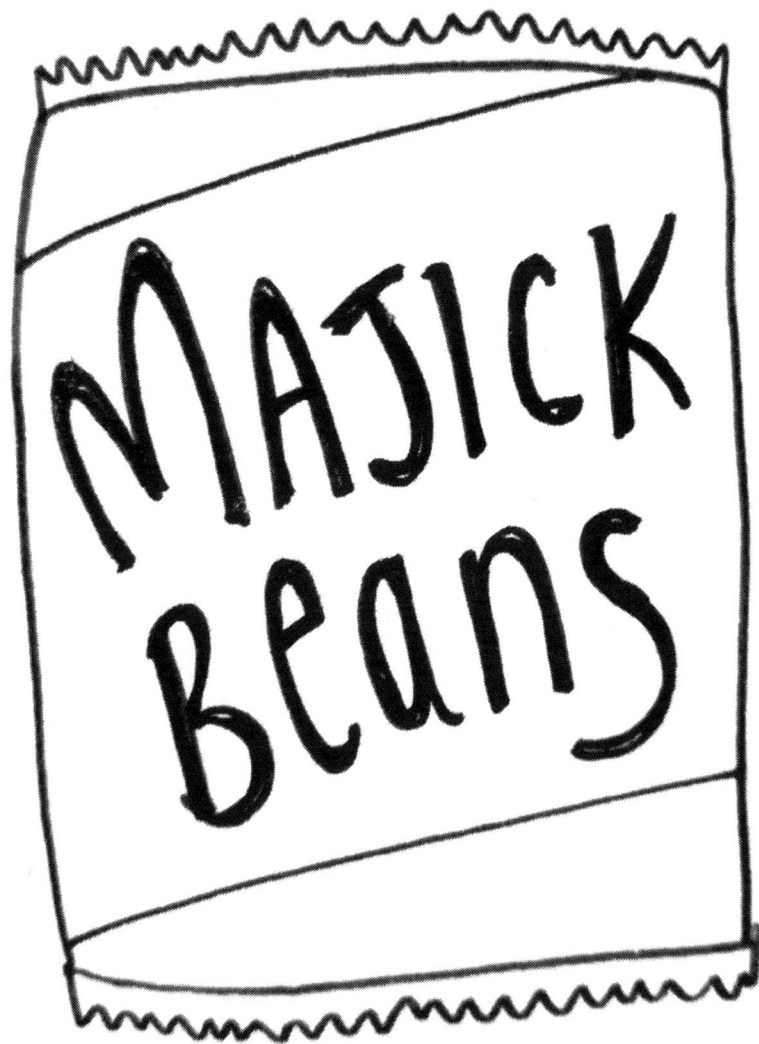

"Wow!" said Jack. "That sounds like a great deal and absolutely believable, sold!"

"YOU ABSOLUTE DIPSHIT. WHAT HAVE YOU DONE!?" screamed Jack's mum, when he returned home. "Magic beans? MAGIC BEANS?? WHAT AM I GOING TO DO WITH MAGIC BEANS?"

Sharon got up from her chair, grabbed the beans from Jack's hand, stormed out of the room and threw them into the small box room on her way out of the front door.

Several days later Jack woke up late, swinging his legs over the side of his bed he shuffled to the bathroom for a wazz. On the way he noticed something odd. There was a strong smell coming from the box room. Not the normal shitty, farmyard smell from Nigel but something more... herby.

He cracked open the door and was shocked by what he saw. One of the beans had taken root in a large cow pat and had grown so much that it was now out of the window! He shouted his mum.

"MUM, MUM. COME AND SEE THIS!"

There was no answer.

"MUUUUUUUUUUMMMMM!"

"Jesus Christ Jack. It's 11.45 AM! Why on earth are you shouting me at this ungodly hour?"
"I think you'll want to see this," replied Jack.

So, Sharon groggily sauntered into the box room and yawned.

"All I can see is cow shit, more cow shit and

HOLY FUCKING CRAP

that's the biggest weed plant I've seen in my entire life!"

Jack was slightly taken aback that she seemed so excited about a weed. If anything he thought she would be angry. The last time she did any gardening was when she had to dig a 6 inch hole to bury his pet budgie, Tyson.

"Weed as in cannabis you soppy twat. We're going to be rich!"

They both looked out the window and were astounded to see that it reached up and up and up into the clouds.

"Jack, get your shoes on and get up that weedstalk pronto. I want to know exactly how tall that bad boy is. And get some of the big leaves from the top while you're there."

"Why do I have to do it?" protested Jack. It's flipping massive!"

"I thought boys were supposed to like climbing things, just don't look down. You'll be fine."

So, Jack tentatively put one foot up onto the window sill and lifted himself up and out into the fresh air and clung onto the stalk for dear life. Poor Jack was shaking like a shitting dog.

Slowly he began to climb the stalk. Up and up it went all the way into the clouds. He must have been half a mile up by now and he was freaking out. The only thing that kept him going was that the risk of falling to his certain death was preferable to facing up to his mum empty handed.

On and on he went until finally he emerged from the clouds and saw a huge castle in the sky.

"OMG!"

Jack didn't say, not being an American teenager, or an annoying twat.

"That reminds me of the cheesy year 2000 dance hit by Ian Van Dahl, erm, 'Castles in the sky'" he also didn't say, having never heard of them due to not being born until 2014.

Clambering to the very top of the weedstalk, Jack jumped off onto the cloud. Up close the castle was absolutely mahoosive. The front door was the size of Jack's entire tower block. He noticed that there was a gap under the door big enough for him to stoop under so he scurried inside.

The first thing he saw was a huge tree trunk, the biggest he had ever seen. Slowly, he craned his neck skywards and realised it was not a tree, but a chair leg.

Suddenly he heard a booming voice...

"FEE - FI - FO - FUM,
I SMELL THE BLOOD OF AN ENGLISHMAN,
BOY, GIRL, WOMAN, TRANS, INTERSEX OR
NON-BINARY PERSON*, I CAN'T REALLY TELL.
BE HE/SHE/THEY ALIVE OR DEAD,
I'LL GRIND HIS/HER/THEIR BONES
TO MAKE MY BREAD."

*THE GIANT HAD RECENTLY BEEN ON A GENDER AWARENESS COURSE.

Jack shat his pants.

It was the loudest thing he had heard in his entire life and left his ears ringing.

He quickly ran to the corner of the room and hid in a hole in the skirting board. He breathed a sigh of relief, thinking that he would be safe. Until he turned around and saw a mouse the size of an elephant. He promptly shat himself once more and let out a squeal.

Fortunately the squeal was so high pitched that the giant didn't even register it.

Jack ran alongside the skirting board as fast as his little legs would carry him, which was not very.

The giant stood up and crashed towards him.

Jack quickly darted into a shadow and stayed as still as he possibly could.

It seemed to work as the giant waved his fist in frustration. As he did so Jack saw something glint in the light. It was a huge, gold sovereign ring that must've been as big as Jack's head.

Now Jack didn't know very much about gold but he thought to himself 'given that the current price of gold on the UK market is roughly £41.96 per gram and estimating that the ring weighs around 400 grams then I calculate it to be worth, on the open market, approximately £fuckingloadsofmoney. Or I could just sell it at Cash Converters for £3.75' thought Jack.

'I have to get my hands on it,' he thought.

The booming voice then returned, nearly sending Jack sideways.

"WHAT'S FOR TEA WIFE*?"

thundered the giant.

"I DON'T KNOW, WHY DON'T YOU GO AND SEE FOR YOURSELF? WHAT DID YOUR LAST SLAVE DIE OF?"

came the equally loud, but *slightly* higher pitched voice.

"WHAT, BRIAN? I FLOGGED HIM TO DEATH LAST TUESDAY BECAUSE HE LEFT A USED TEABAG ON THE SIDE, REMEMBER?"

*THE COURSE HADN'T BEEN THAT SUCCESSFUL

"OH YEAH," said the giant's wife, who we'll call Betty, because that was her name.

"WE'VE GOT SOME OF THOSE RUSTLERS BURGERS FROM B AND M BARGAINS?" offered Betty.

"BOSTIN, I'LL HAVE 25 OF THEM THEN, I'M ONLY A LITTLE BIT PECKISH. TAKE THE EDGE OFF UNTIL TEA TIME NICELY THAT WILL." 'What a greedy bastard.' thought Jack.

After the microwaved had pinged 25 times and the giant had gorged himself, making some disgusting noises in the process (these noises reminded Jack of the noises coming from his mum's bedroom when 'Uncle John' comes over. Maybe they like Rustlers burgers as well?) the giant promptly fell into a deep sleep.

This is my chance. thought Jack. *It's now or never.*

Quietly, Jack ran over towards the giant, who was slumped over the table. He clambered up the chair leg and onto the giant's lap.

He grabbed the material of the giant's clothing and ran down the length of his arm and onto his hand. The back of the giant's hand was like a forest of greasy black hair. Jack arrived at the ring and up close it looked even bigger. He started to pull at the ring with all his might, keeping an eye out for Betty and to make sure that the giant didn't wake up. He didn't stir and continued to snore like a foghorn.

Heaving at the ring, Jack felt it shift on the giant's finger. With one final, almighty pull it came free and crashed onto the floor.

Jack closed his eyes and gritted his teeth, sure that this would wake the giant. When he opened his eyes he breathed a sigh of relief realising the giant was still sleeeping soundly.

He ran back down the giant's clothing, where he noticed a label that said 'George'. 'Ah, so that must be his name.' thought Jack. Once back on the kitchen floor Jack retrieved the gold ring, and made for the exit.

Jack scrambled back under the door and jumped down onto the beanstalk, just remembering to pick a bag full of the cannabis leaves which he slung over his back before starting the big climb down.

It was no easy task holding onto a massive gold ring, a huge bag of weed and having hands free to hold on for dear life.

After about an hour of climbing his tower block came into view. Wondering how his mum would react to his spoils, he climbed back in through his window.

"JACK, WHAT HAVE I TOLD YOU ABOUT STEALING?" said Sharon when she saw what Jack had brought home.

Jack looked confused.

"B-b-b-but?"

"Steal as much as you can carry you dweeb! One ring? If he's got that then surely he's got more. First thing tomorrow morning you're straight back up that weedstalk!"

So, early the next morning Jack was back on the weedstalk and before too long back in the castle.

He rooted around looking for more valuables and before long he struck gold, when he, erm, struck gold. He wasn't sure what it was but it looked like a ring with 2 balls on it. It said something like 'Prince Albert' on it.

Jack shoved it in his sack and scarpered. But as he reached the door he felt a large shadow cast over him.

"I'VE GOT YOU NOW YOU LITTLE LAND LUBBER!" he cried.

"AND WHAT ARE YOU DOING WITH MY COCK PIERCING, YOU LITTLE PERVO!"

Jack ran for his life. He belted towards the weedstalk, screaming as he did. He stood no chance of out running the giant but George was clumsy and uncoordinated.

Jack reached the stalk and started to shimmy down, with George on the stalk as well it was swinging wildly all over the place.

It was as much as Jack could do just to hold on, but hold on he did. Jack managed to climb down in half the time that it had taken him the day before. When he saw his flat come into view he started to scream to his mum.

"MUM!!!! MUM!!! HELP! The giant is chasing me down!"

Sharon casually looked out of the window and said, "Always the drama queen aren't we?". Taking an axe that she kept for emergencies just like this she swung it and with one hefty blow sliced right through the weedstalk.

"Take that you big giant twat," she said as George came crashing to the ground, sending tremors that could be felt in Timbuktu.

Sharon let Jack catch his breath before setting him to work stripping the stalk clean of leaves. He filled 47 bin bags full of the stuff.

Jack passed his mum the loot, which she reckoned had the street value of a cool million pounds.

"That'll do nicely!" said Sharon.

She made a couple of calls and within the hour she had sold the rings and all of the bags of cannabis to a couple of locally, well respected entreprenuers, called Mad Dog and One Eyed Jim, who assured Sharon that they were fully legit. They even gave her a receipt.

And so Jack and Sharon were rich beyond their wildest dreams. Sharon never had to work another day of her life. I mean, she had never worked a day in her life anyway, but you get my point.

They were able to move out of Grimsville and enjoy life in the affluent suburb of Happytown, where Sharon achieved her lifelong ambition of owning a 250 inch TV, on which to watch Homes Under the Hammer, while chain smoking 4 fags at a time.

The end.

Printed in Great Britain
by Amazon